FAVORITE DOG BREEDS

BEAGLES

by Martha E.H. Rustad

AMICUS HIGH INTEREST • AMICUS INK

Amicus High Interest and Amicus Ink are imprints of Amicus
P.O. Box 227, Mankato, MN 56002
www.amicuspublishing.us

Library of Congress Cataloging-in-Publication Data
Names: Rustad, Martha E. H. (Martha Elizabeth Hillman), 1975- author.
Title: Beagles / by Martha E. H. Rustad.
Description: Mankato, Minnesota : Amicus High Interest/Amicus Ink, [2018] | Series: Favorite dog breeds | Audience: Ages 5-10. | Audience: K to grade 3. | Includes bibliographical references and index.
Identifiers: LCCN 2016033237 (print) | LCCN 2016039796 (ebook) | ISBN 9781681511245 (library binding) | ISBN 9781681521558 (pbk.) | ISBN 9781681512143 (ebook) | ISBN 9781681512143 (pdf)
Subjects: LCSH: Beagle (Dog breed)--Juvenile literature. | Dog breeds--Juvenile literature.
Classification: LCC SF429.B3 R87 2018 (print) | LCC SF429.B3 (ebook) | DDC 636.753/7--dc23
LC record available at https://lccn.loc.gov/2016033237

Photo Credits: Marazem/Dreamstime cover; Ermolaev Alexander/shutterstock 2, 10; igorr1/iStock 5; Paris Pierce/Alamy Stock Photo/Alamy 6-7; AleksandarNakic/iStock 9; Peter Kirillov/shutterstock 12-13; anetapics/shutterstock/PW 14-15; Mark Raycroft/Minden Pictures 17; verity johnson/iStock 18-19; monkeybusinessimages/iStock 21; Akitameldes/shutterstock/PW 22

Editor: Wendy Dieker
Designer: Tracy Myers
Photo Researcher: Aubrey Harper and Holly Young

TABLE OF CONTENTS

ON THE TRAIL

What is that smell? A dog sniffs. She follows the **trail**. Got it! The beagle found her hidden treat. Beagles have good noses.

Furry Fact

Beagles are medium-sized dogs. They are about as tall as a kid's knees.

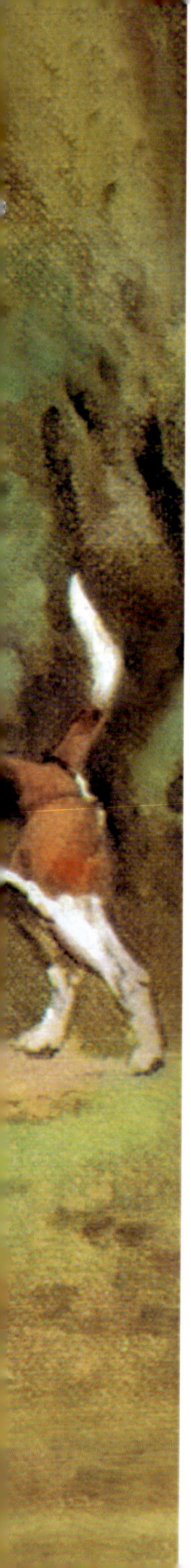

HISTORY

The beagle breed began in Europe. Packs of dogs helped hunters. These **hounds** sniffed prey hundreds of years ago. They were the first beagles.

A NOSE FOR SMELLING

Beagles have strong noses. They remember many smells. Beagles track **scents**. They follow the trail to find what made the smell.

Furry Fact
A beagle can tell the difference among 50 smells.

LONG EARS, SHORT LEGS

A beagle's long ears hang down. Its ears help the dog smell. The ears sweep scents toward the nose. Short legs keep their noses low to the ground.

WHITE-TIPPED TAIL

The tip of a beagle's tail is white. The tail stays up when the dog is sniffing. The tail is easy to spot from far away.

Puppies

About six puppies are born in a **litter**. All the pups in a litter may look different. Some may be black, brown, and white. Others may be just brown and white.

Furry Fact

A beagle puppy's fur color may change. Light fur may turn darker, or spots seem to move around!

BARK! BAY! HOWL!

Beagles are noisy dogs. A friendly bark seems to say hello. Beagles **bay** as they follow a scent trail. This long, low sound tells other beagles to follow. They might howl when they are lonely.

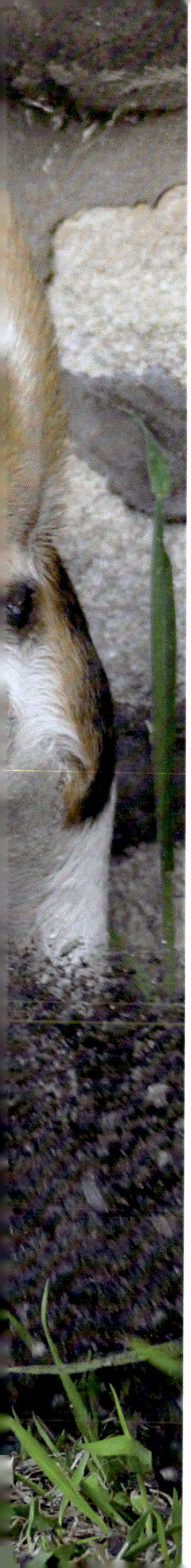

HAPPY TO ROAM

Beagles like to roam. They are happy to follow their noses. Clever beagles find ways to follow tough trails. They will even dig under fences and stone walls!

FAMILY DOG

Beagles are good family dogs. They like to be part of a group. A family is a good group for a beagle. Beagles make great pets.

HOW DO YOU KNOW IT'S A BEAGLE?

WORDS TO KNOW

bay – to make a long, low sound; beagles bay to alert other beagles to a scent trail

hound – a hunting dog

litter – a group of puppies born at the same time

scent – a smell

trail – a line of smells left behind by an animal

LEARN MORE

Books

Bodden, Valerie. *Beagles*. Fetch! Mankato, Minn.: Creative Education, 2014.

Schuh, Mari. *Beagles*. Blastoff! Readers: Awesome Dogs. Minneapolis: Bellwether Media, 2016.

Websites

American Kennel Club: The Beagle
http://www.akc.org/dog-breeds/beagle/

Animal Planet Dogs 101: Beagle
http://www.animalplanet.com/tv-shows/dogs-101/videos/beagle/

INDEX